"A young girl walking on water… that only exists in fairy tales.
Yet, the vast ocean is truly a "magical" place.
So, join Mina on her journey and meet the creatures that live
in the sea. Listen carefully to what they have to say and you'll be
amazed by the incredible stories they have to tell.
They will also teach you lots of wonderful things."

François Sarano

General Manager: Gauthier Auzou
Graphic Design: Eloïse Jensen
Production: Lucile Pierret
Translation from French: Steve Gadler
©Auzou Publishing, Paris (France), 2015 (English version).
ISBN: 978-2-7338-3599-9

Printed and bound in China, July 2015

The Little Girl
Who Walked on Water

— but didn't know how to swim —

By François Sarano · Illustration by Marion Sarano

AUZOU

Once upon a time, a long time ago, there was a small island lost
in the middle of a huge ocean. There was nobody around for miles.
Yet, everyone lived on the island happily.

The reason was because under the surface of the ocean, there was
the most beautiful, the most abundant, and the most colorful reefs.
Vibrant fish swam in the clear water. Shellfish, crabs, and shrimp
scurried across the ocean floor. Their brilliant colors mingled like
a rainbow in the sky.

The islanders had no reason to worry.
They spent hours watching the wonders of the ocean while their
children swam in pursuit of playful dolphins and rays.

It was the island of happiness and everyone enjoyed it.

Everyone?

Well, not really…

On the beach, a little girl sat by herself and sobbed.
This little girl dreamed of exploring the depths of the ocean.

Her name was Mina and she was born with a gift both
extraordinary and terrible: she could walk on water!
But, she couldn't swim under the sea. She floated like a cork!

She could run and dance on the waves. But, she couldn't
dive with her friends and swim with the fish. Instead of taking
advantage of her exceptional talent, Mina spent her days
in tears of disappointment.

Everyday, Mina would dive into the waves and try to sink into the sea. But everyday, she would float back up to the surface and drift along the surf.

Mina tried everything! She jumped into the water with a belt made of stones. She crawled into the breakers clinging to rocks.

But nothing worked. Mina still floated like a cork!

Alone on the beach, Mina cried. She cried so much that
a nearby crab thought the tide was coming in and climbed
out of his burrow.

"You can't swim?" asked the crab. "Big deal!

You can jump over the waves. Enjoy it! Just like you, I have
something to complain about. I look straight ahead, but I walk
sideways, which isn't always easy. I scramble over the rocks and
find hiding places with my feet. I am content with who I am.

So, I will help you."

The crab used his big pincers to pull Mina under the water.
He squeezed and squeezed.

But it didn't work. Mina still floated like a cork!

Mina screamed and yelled in frustration and attracted the attention of a nearby octopus gliding between the corals.

"Why are you complaining?" asked the octopus.
"You can't swim? Big deal!

Just like you, I have something to complain about. My body is so soft that despite my eight legs, I can't stand up straight. So I use my soft body to slip into the smallest holes. I am content with who I am.

So, I will help you."

The octopus used his eight legs to pull Mina under the water.
He pulled and pulled.

But it didn't work. Mina still floated like a cork!

So, Mina decided to go far, far away.

She walked onto the ocean and glided along the crest of the waves.

But, Mina didn't enjoy it.

Behind a large wave, Mina saw a beautiful white fin slicing through the water's surface.

"You're a funny fish!" said Mina. "I would really like to be like you."

"I'm a sunfish," the strange fish replied. "You really would like to look like me? Big deal!

Just like you I have something to complain about. I'm round like the sun and I don't have a tail, just a big fin on my back and another on my belly. To swim, I lie flat and use my fins like wings. It's not always easy, but I am content with who I am.

So, I will help you."

The sunfish showed Mina how to wave her arms like fins.
She waved and waved.

But it didn't work. Mina still floated like a cork!

Mina was so tired. She sat down on the water and fell fast asleep.
Joyful whistles woke her from her slumber!

"Why are you so far from your parents?" asked the dolphin.
"You can't swim? Big deal!

Just like you I have something to complain about. I can't breathe
under water like fish, I have to breathe in the open air! It doesn't
make it easy to sleep. When one side is sleeping, the other side
is awake! But I'm content with who I am.

So, I will help you."

The dolphin told Mina to hold on tight while he dove deep
into the ocean. He dove deeper and deeper.

But it didn't work.
Mina still floated like a cork!

Mina went on her way. Just below the surface, she saw a dazzling, bright creature.

"Why did you leave the family who love you so much?" asked the jellyfish. "You can't swim? Big deal!

My ancestors were here millions and millions of years ago. And I still don't have any friends! I'm delicate and fragile and I sting to survive. People are frightened of me. It's not fair! But I'm content with who I am!

So, I will help you.

The jellyfish tugged Mina below the surface. He tugged and tugged.

But it didn't work. Mina still floated like a cork!

The island was just a speck on the horizon when a fish
with wings flew by!

"Why are you crying?" asked the flying fish. "You can't swim?
Big deal!

I'd like to run on water like you! But, I'm stuck here in the open
sea, and I have no place to hide. But I'm content with who I am!
When I fly over the water, I dream that I'm a bird.

So, I will help you."

The flying fish showed Mina how to flap her arms like wings.
She flapped and flapped.

But it didn't work. Mina still floated like a cork!

The sky began to darken when Mina came upon a small island.

"Watch where you're going!" shouted a large turtle. "You can't swim? Big deal!

Just like you I have something to complain about. I live at sea, I eat at sea, and I sleep at sea. But, I must lay my eggs on land! It takes me hours to crawl on the beach. Then, I have to return to the sea before the sun dries my shell. But, I am happy with who I am.

So, I will help you."

The turtle showed Mina how to crawl through the water. She crawled and crawled.

But, it didn't work. Mina still floated like a cork!

Mina didn't know what to do.

No matter what she tried, Mina still floated like a cork!

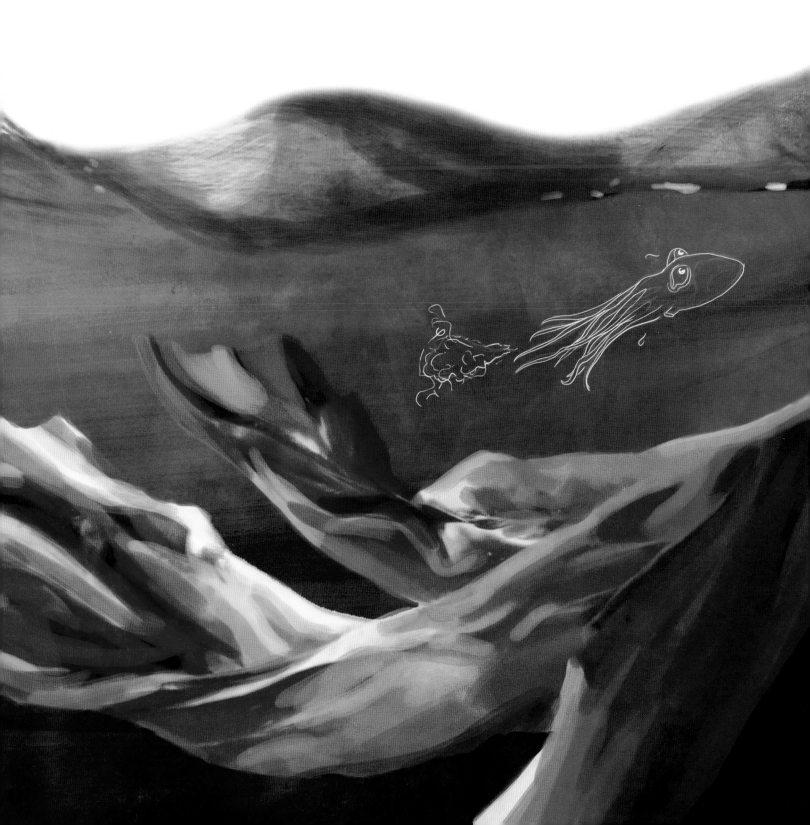

A storm brewed over the ocean. Rain poured down, and finally,
Mina was swallowed by the sea. She struggled and struggled
to rise to the surface.

But, this time, nothing worked—Mina sank deeper and deeper!

"Ocean, please give me a second chance," Mina pleaded.
"If you save me, I promise to be happy as I am."

So, the ocean changed Mina's legs into fins and allowed
her to breathe in the water.

Mina was a mermaid!

She swam better than dolphins, faster than fish, and deeper
than the whales.

But soon, Mina was thinking about her little brother, her parents,
and her village. Once again, sadness overwhelmed her.

With a flip of her fins, Mina swam back to the island.

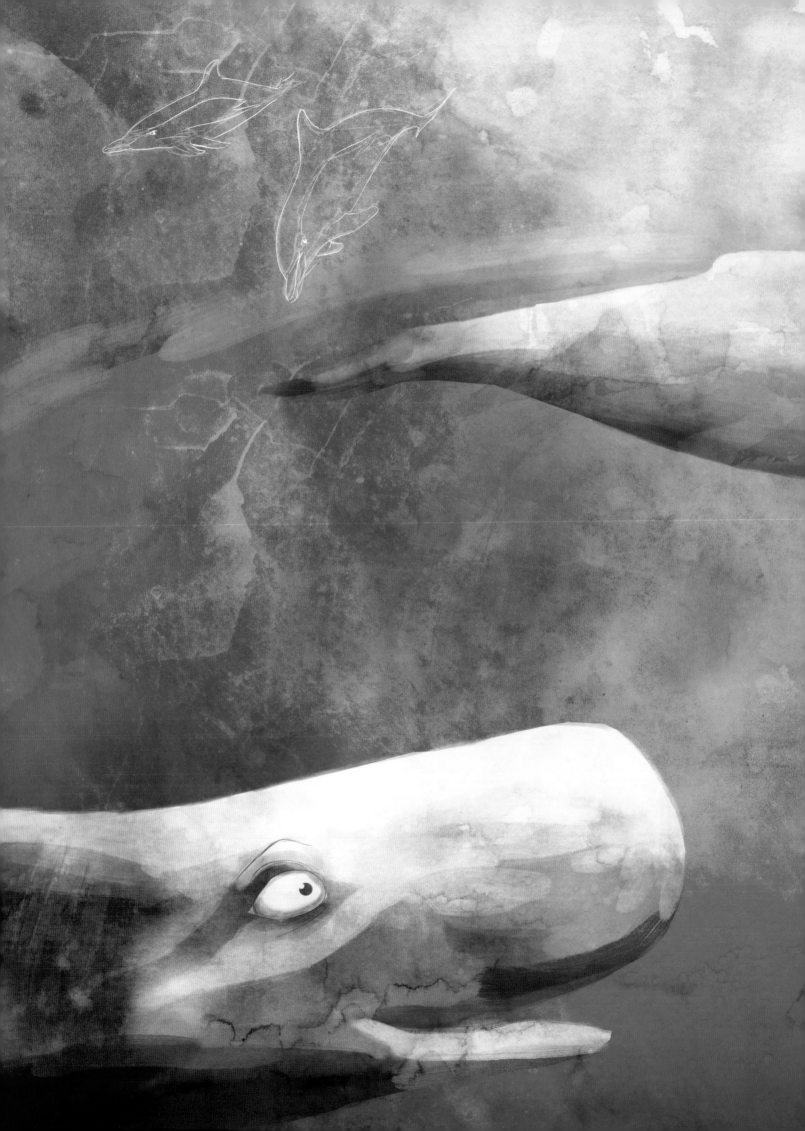

As she approached the shore, Mina became worried.
She promised the ocean she would be happy. But now that
her legs were covered with scales and her feet were fins,
how could she run toward her brother?

Wondering what to do, Mina looked at the ocean. For the very
first time, she was determined to accept her fate. With as much
courage as she could muster, she tried to stand on her fins.
Then the ocean, in all its generosity, gave back her legs.

Mina ran laughing to the village.

Every day since then, Mina, the little girl who walks on water,
takes her brother and his friends to play beyond the reef.
And if you listen carefully, beyond the foam and the crashing
waves, you can hear Mina laughing.

And, every full moon, Mina becomes a mermaid
and swims in the ocean that gave back her joy!